Which Way
to the Revolution?

A Book About Maps

Bob Barner

Two lights in
the Old North Church.

The British
are coming!

Holiday House
New York

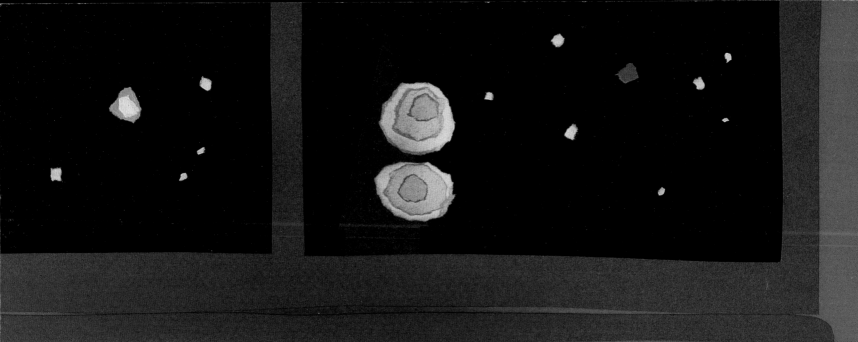

Library of Congress Cataloging-in-Publication Data

Barner, Bob.
    Which way to the revolution? : a book about maps / Bob Barner, —
1st   ed.
        p.   cm.
    Summary: Text and maps describe the route traveled by Paul Revere
when he warned the colonists of the approach of the British prior to
the outbreak of the American Revolution.
    ISBN: 0-8234-1352-7 (HC)
    1. Revere, Paul, 1735-1818—Juvenile literature. 2. Map reading—
Massachusetts—Juvenile literature. 3. Massachusetts—History—Revolution,
1775-1783—Maps—Juvenile literature. 4. United States—History–Revolution,
1775-1783—Maps-Juvenile literature. [1. Revere, Paul, 1735-1818. 2. Map
reading. 3. Maps. 4. Massachusetts—History—Revolution 1775-1783.
5. United States—History—Revolution, 1775-1783.] I. Title.
E216.B37 1998   97-34043
                                                                CIP
                                                                AC

For Belle Akers and Ellen Becker-Gray,
my two favorite teachers

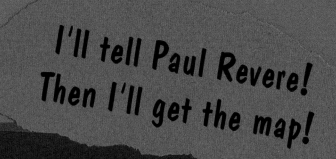

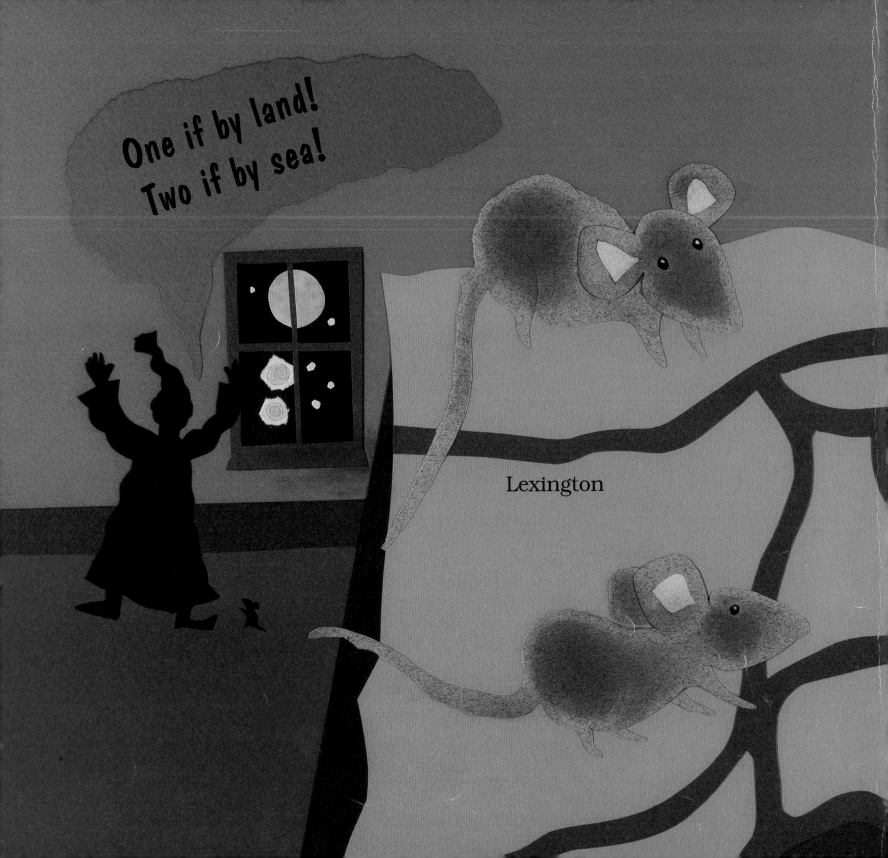

The British are coming! Tonight Paul Revere must travel far to warn people. Here is the map.

Medford

Mystic River

N

W E

S

Old Oak Tree

Wooden Bridge

Cambridge

Bunker Hill

Charlestown

Now follow his route.

Boston Harbor

Charles River

Boston

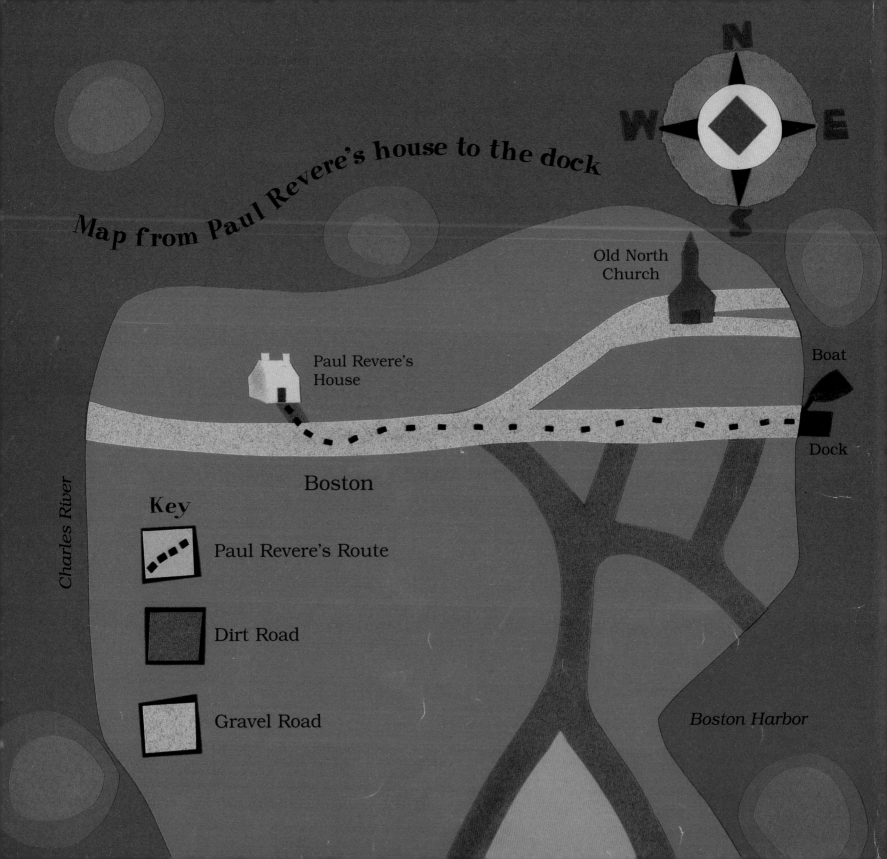

First, we run east and head for the dock.
A boat's the only way to cross Boston Harbor.

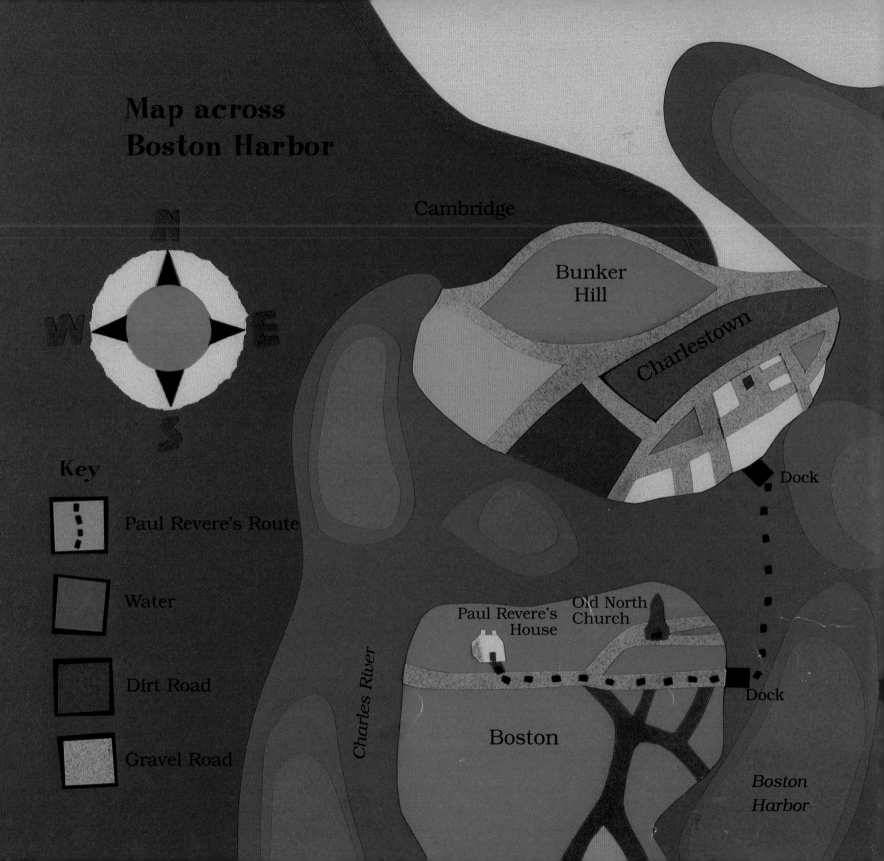

We row straight north to Charlestown.

It looks like we're lost,

but our map will show the way. North to Bunker Hill!

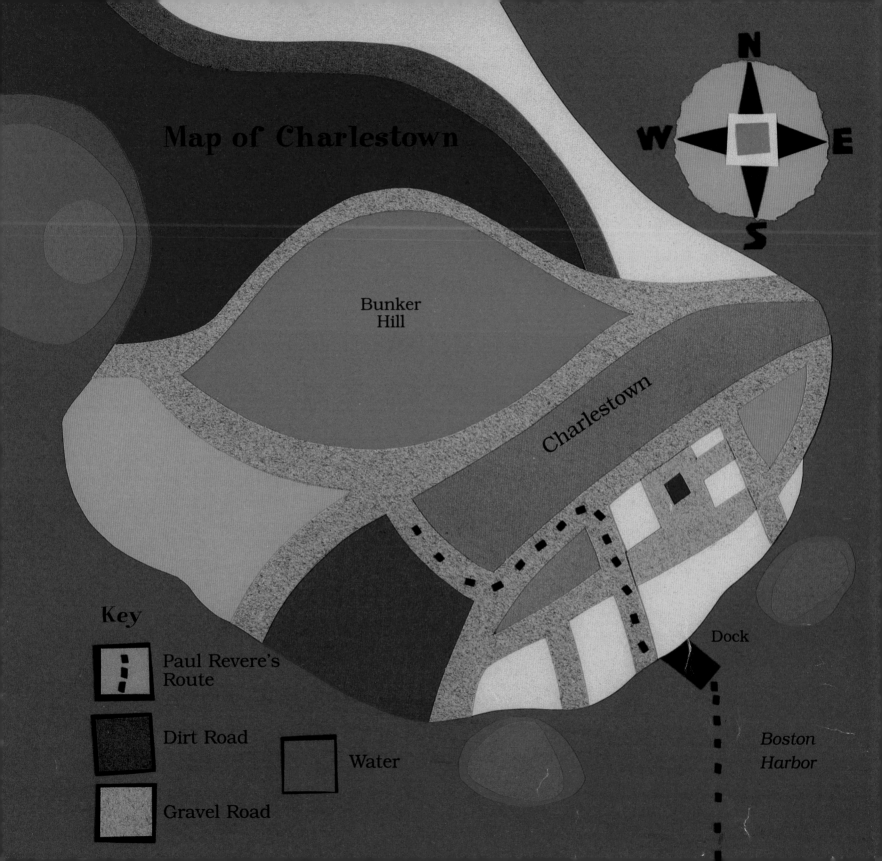

Map of Charlestown

Bunker
Hill

Charlestown

Dock

*Boston
Harbor*

Key

Paul Revere's
Route

Dirt Road

Water

Gravel Road

We gallop up Bunker Hill and straight down the other side.
Not a problem in sight until we see . . . .

Big nasty rats!

They scare horses,

break bridges,

and put stones in the street.

They turn signs,

chew on ropes,

and dig holes in the road.

BOSTON

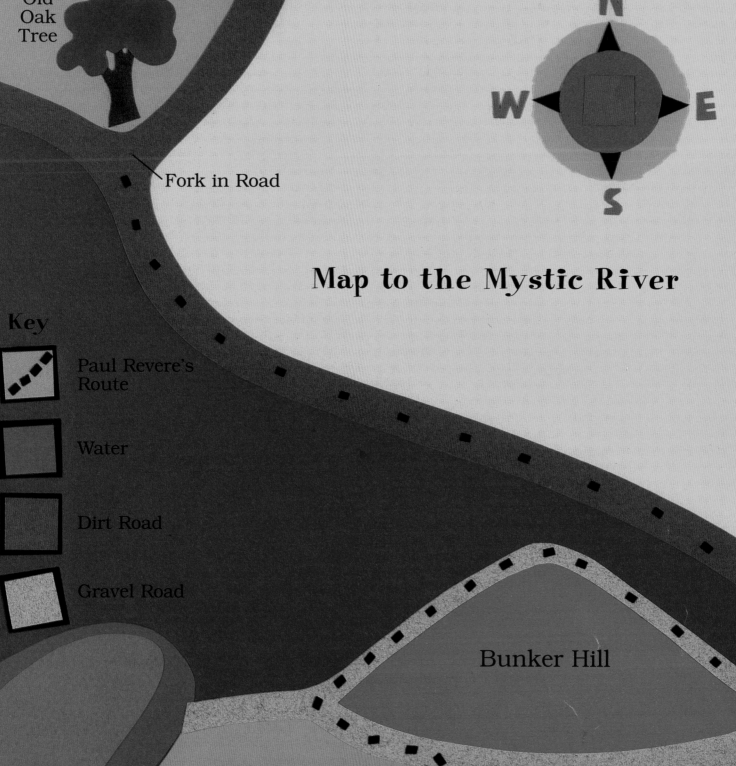

Old
Oak
Tree

N

W   E

S

Fork in Road

Map to the Mystic River

Key

Paul Revere's
Route

Water

Dirt Road

Gravel Road

Bunker Hill

Rats! We look at our map so we can't be fooled. We'll turn right at the sign by the big Old Oak Tree. Then on to the Mystic River.

Cross over the new wooden bridge.

Head north toward the town of Medford.

Rats have turned the signs! But we keep checking our map.

To go to Medford, we stay north at the fork in the road.

Map to Medford

Medford

Mystic River

Wooden
Bridge

Key

 Paul Revere's Route

 Dirt Road

Water

Old
Oak
Tree

N

W E

S

Fork in Road

At last we're in Medford and trot right through town. The rats don't look happy.

What a ride! From Boston to Charlestown, from Medford to Lexington, we followed our map!

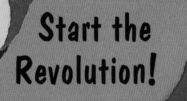

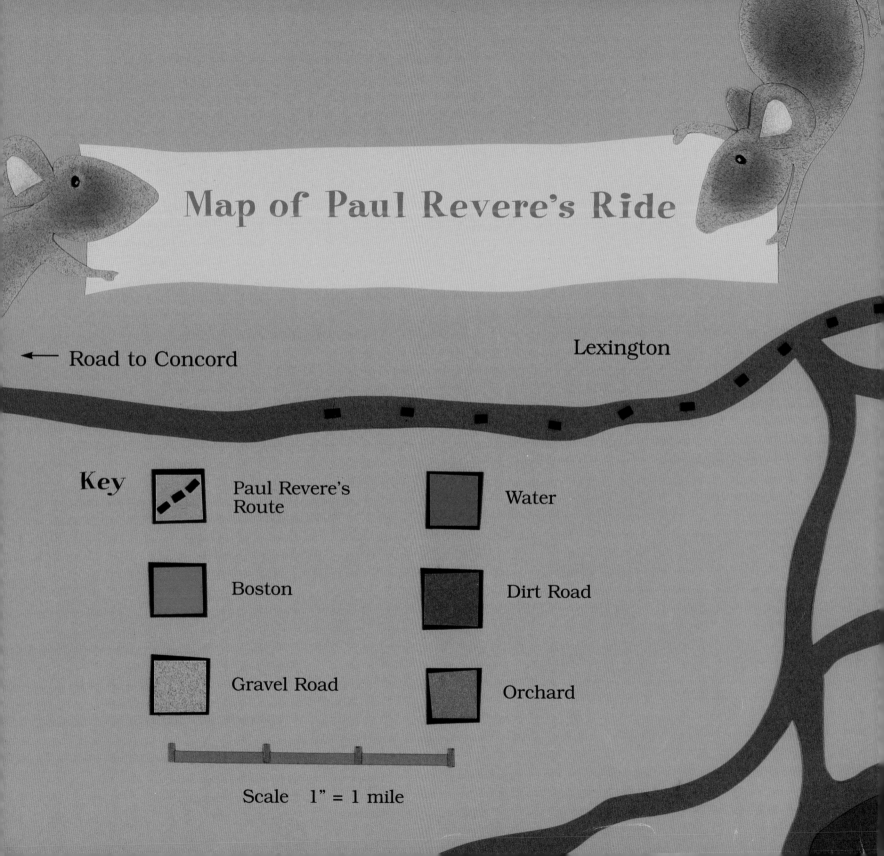

Map of Paul Revere's Ride

← Road to Concord

Lexington

Key

- Paul Revere's Route
- Water
- Boston
- Dirt Road
- Gravel Road
- Orchard

Scale   1" = 1 mile

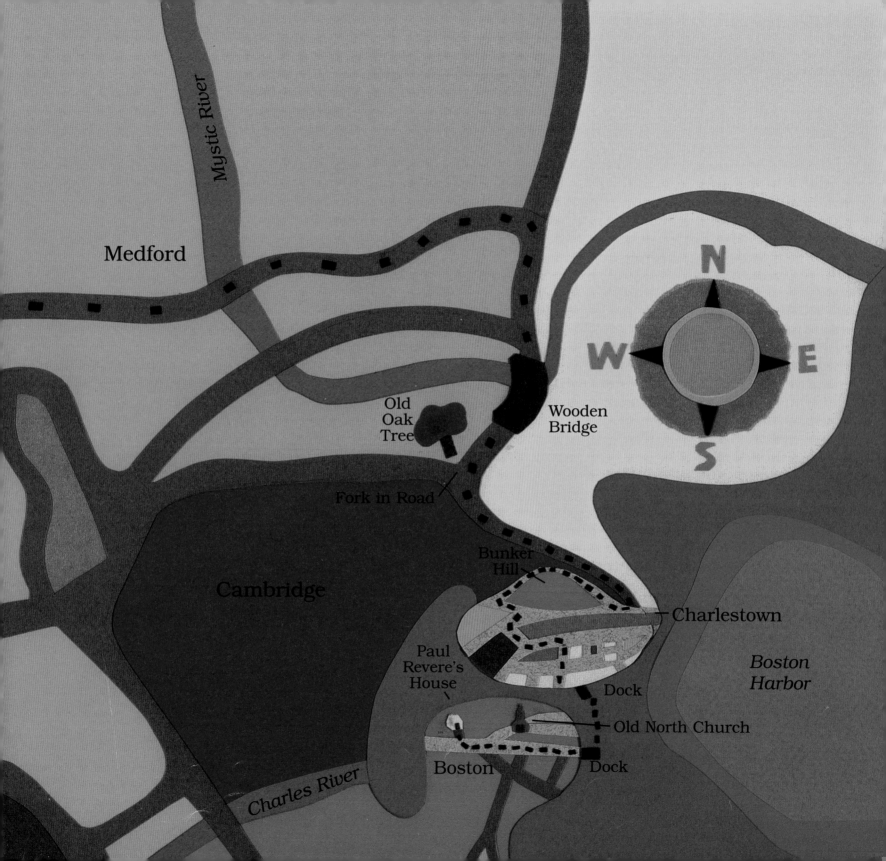

Map Notes

Now that you've read this book you can make a map of your room, your house, your school, your neighborhood, or even a map of the entire country or planet. Use the things listed below to make your map clear and easy to follow.

Compass Rose—The top of a compass rose always points north on a map to show the position of places and things on the map.

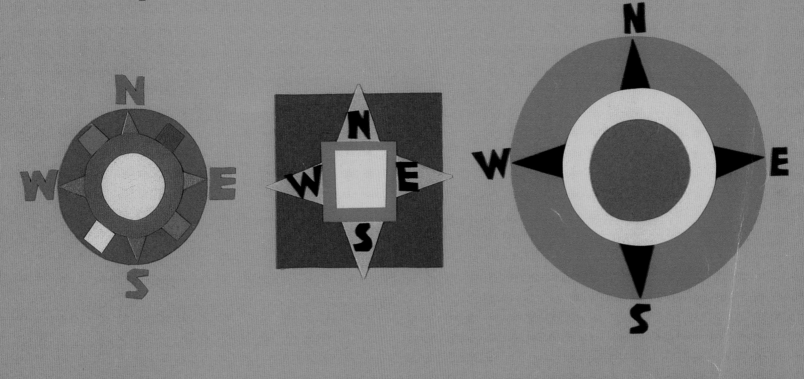

Map Key—Shapes, samples, or colors used to show what is in each area of a map are part of the map key.

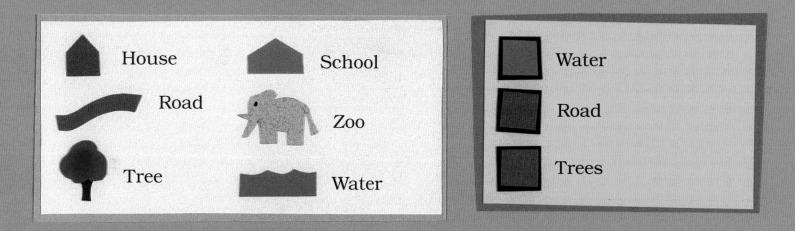

Scale—A map scale shows how much real distance is represented by a distance shown on the map.

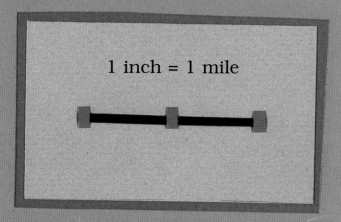

Paul Revere's Ride

We'll never know if Paul Revere had mice in his house in Boston, Massachusetts. But we do know that on the night of April 18, 1775, he made his famous ride from Boston to Lexington to warn people about the British troops.

Paul Revere lived in Boston and worked as a silversmith making teapots, spoons, and cups by hand out of silver. Like most people in Boston, Paul Revere didn't like being ruled by the British government. There were many British troops staying in Boston. Paul Revere had a plan. If more British troops came to Boston by the land route, one light would shine in the Old North Church steeple. If they came by sea, two lights would shine to signal the start of his ride. "One if by land, two if by sea."

Although Paul Revere was captured by British troops before he reached Concord, he had warned many patriots about the coming British army. The battles of Lexington and Concord that took place on April 19, 1775 started the American Revolution. Paul Revere is still well-known today because Henry Wadsworth Longfellow wrote a famous poem about him.

Paul Revere probably used maps and landmarks like trees, bridges, signs, and water to find his way. As far as we know, he made the trip without the help of a mouse.